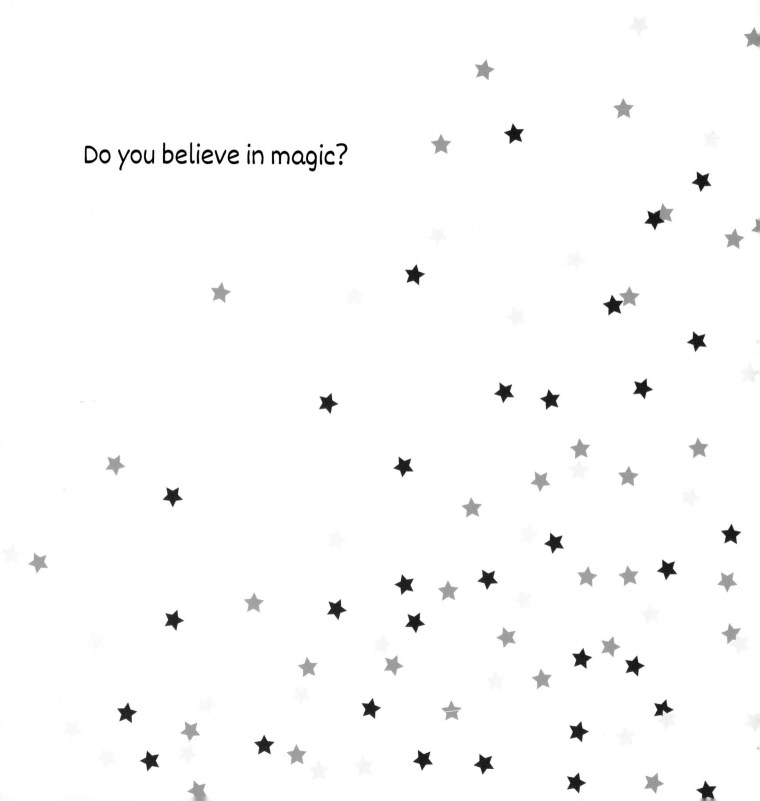

Do you believe in magic?

For my two stars.
The inspiration for this journey.

A CIP catalogue record for this book is available from the British library.

ISBN: 978-1-7397701-0-5

Printed in the UK.

William the Wizard's Wonky Wand

Written by Scott Fleming
Illustrated by Patrycja Paczkowska

In a magical land not far away . . .

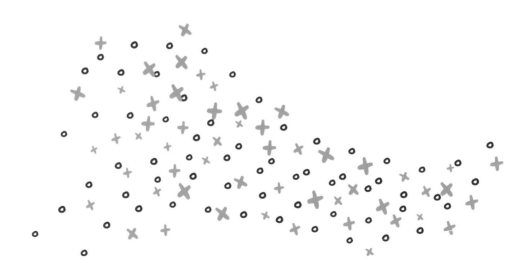

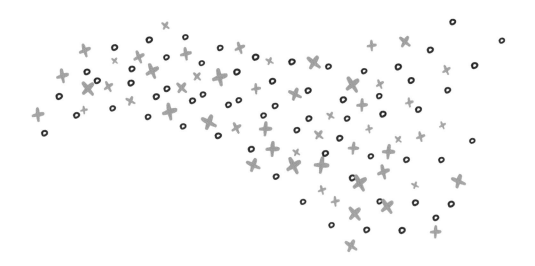

...a magical family live and play.

This is William.
He is eight years old and training to be a wizard.

William likes using magic to help people, and in his spare time,
he has been practising a spell that turns broccoli into ice cream.
But there is one little problem . . .

. . . William the Wizard has a wonky wand!

He was given a training wand when he turned five years old
and has to use it until he learns responsible magic.
But the family training wand is grumpy and old,
and quite often it doesn't do as it's told.

One day, William and his friend Archie went for a walk through the old forest. They were looking for a reep, which is a large green magical rabbit that makes a noise like a baby elephant.

Archie was hoping to see a reep for the first time,
but it started to rain, and reeps don't like rain.
Archie's jacket didn't have a hood and his feet were getting cold.

"Don't worry," said William, "I'll take care of this.

Wand, wand, do your best magic yet.
Stop my friend from getting wet."

"OH NO!" said Archie.

"Instead of putting a hat on my head,
your wonky wand has gone and put bread!"

William tried again to help Archie.

"Come on wand, I said do your best magic yet.
Please stop my friend from getting wet."

"OH NO!" said Archie.

"Instead of giving me a pair of cosy wellies,
your wonky wand covered my boots with jellies!"

William was getting a little bit frustrated with his wand now.

"Wand, wand, please try again.
Protect my friend from the falling rain."

"OH NO!" said Archie.

"Instead of giving me a waterproof jacket,
your wonky wand gave me a tennis racket!"

The wand was not behaving and William did not like it one bit.

Fizz

"Wand, wand, try once more.
Shelter Archie from this heavy downpour."

"OH NO!" said Archie.

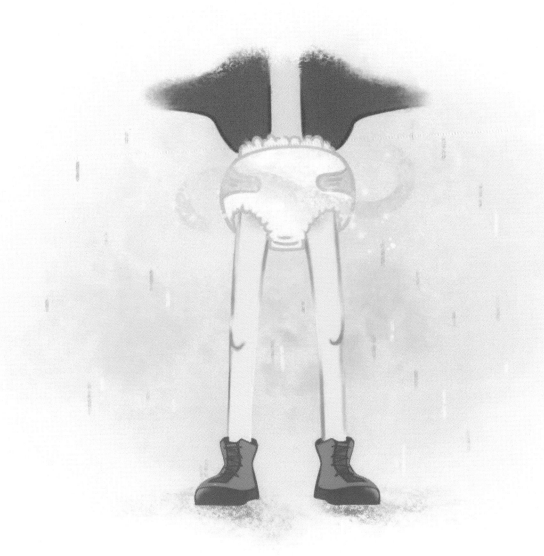

"Instead of making me warm and happy,
your wonky wand turned my jeans into a nappy!"

William just wanted his wand to do one good spell to help his friend, but instead it was being naughty and was starting to make him a little bit angry.

"Wand, you're not working and I don't know why.
Take us both home where it's nice and dry."

"OH NO!" squeaked Archie.

"Instead of taking us back to the house,
your wonky wand changed me into a mouse!"

William was fed up of his wand's wonky behaviour
and was about to give up and start walking back,
when he heard a whoosh followed by a crack!

Whoosh

Crack

William's mum used her magic to bring them back to the house,
and thankfully Archie was no longer a mouse!

"I'm proud of you," she said, "for trying to keep your friend dry.
Especially when your wand wouldn't behave, try after try."

William's mum decided that he had earned a special reward.

"You have studied hard and been responsible too.
Here is a grown-up wand all shiny and new."

"The training wand will now go to another.
Please pass it on to your little brother."

William's brother is a little bit cheeky and naughty as well.
Will the wonky wand help him to play tricks on people?
Only time will tell . . .

what's your wizard name?

Use the month you were born in and the first letter of your first name to reveal your silly wizard name:

Which month were you born in?

January	-	Fibalot
February	-	Shazam
March	-	Yazoo
April	-	Merlin
May	-	Abracadabra
June	-	Bigboss
July	-	Starface
August	-	Willow
September	-	Littleboss
October	-	Calypso
November	-	Hocuspocus
December	-	Minion

What's the first letter of your first name?

A	-	Cracklebottom	N	-	Elfontheshelf
B	-	Dumblefluffle	O	-	Yellowsnow
C	-	The Flatulant	P	-	The Invisible
D	-	Sparkleface	Q	-	Jellybean
E	-	Burpalot	R	-	Thunderpants
F	-	Ticklesocks	S	-	Chucklebum
G	-	Gotobed	T	-	Kissmonkey
H	-	Twinklepump	U	-	McPoopface
I	-	Bogiepicker	V	-	Purplebottom
J	-	Tumblefuzz	W	-	Wonkywand
K	-	Doritomuncher	X	-	Snotcatcher
L	-	Picklebreath	Y	-	Peepeetree
M	-	Chocochomper	Z	-	Huffleshuffle

My wizard name is: --

Coming Soon . . .

William the Wizard's Little Brother's Wonky Wand

William and Freddy's Halloween Surprise

William the Wizard Saves Christmas

 scottfleming_author

 Scott Fleming Author

 @Scottfleming_

 Scott Fleming Author

SCOTTFLEMING_AUTHOR

www.scottflemingauthor.com

Also available from the author:

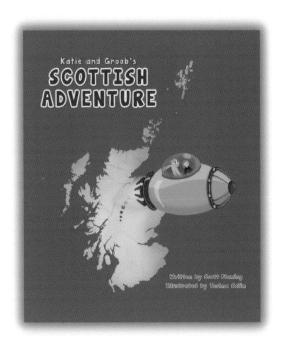

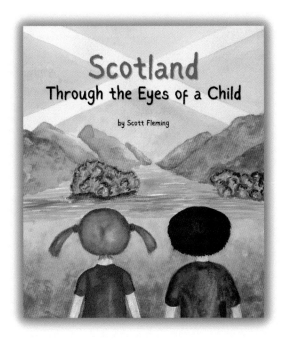

When Katie's gran gives her a book about Scotland, she goes on a fantastic adventure around the country with an inquisitive, friendly alien called Groob.

Scotland as viewed by children. This charity book features a combination of beautiful illustrations and over 100 drawings from primary school children.

Available directly from the author, Amazon, and all good bookshops.
Free activity sheets are also available for all children's books by the author.